Eddie
and Dog

by Alison Brown

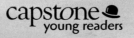
capstone
young readers

He imagined flying to **far-off places** and doing **amazing things**.

Then one day . . .

. . . someone appeared who was looking for
adventure too. He walked up to Eddie.
Eddie asked if he wanted to play.

He did.

EXIT

Together they hunted for **crocodiles** . . . and sailed the **seven seas**.

They built a secret
fortress . . .

and explored a
faraway jungle.

But when they got home, Eddie's mom said the dog couldn't stay because they didn't have a big yard. He would not be happy, stuck inside all day.

So he **had to go.**

Eddie couldn't stop thinking about him.

The dog must have thought about
Eddie, too. Because the next day . . .

he came **back**.

Eddie's mom couldn't believe it!
But she said they had to find him
a better home – one with a big yard.

Eddie didn't think there
was anything wrong with
his home.

The dog must have thought the same.

Because three days later,

to Eddie's delight . . .

he came back.

Eddie's mom took the dog to stay in the country. She said he would be happy there.

Eddie didn't think so.

Eddie was alone again.

He wondered

if the

dog was

missing him

too.

Then, later that night,
Eddie heard a noise.

It was the dog.

He had come **back!**

The dog had a plan.

It was a good plan . . .

. . . a yard on the roof!

Eddie's mom loved it. She said the dog could live with them. He'd be happy now.

Eddie was happy too. His friend was here to stay . . .

. . . and it was time for adventure!

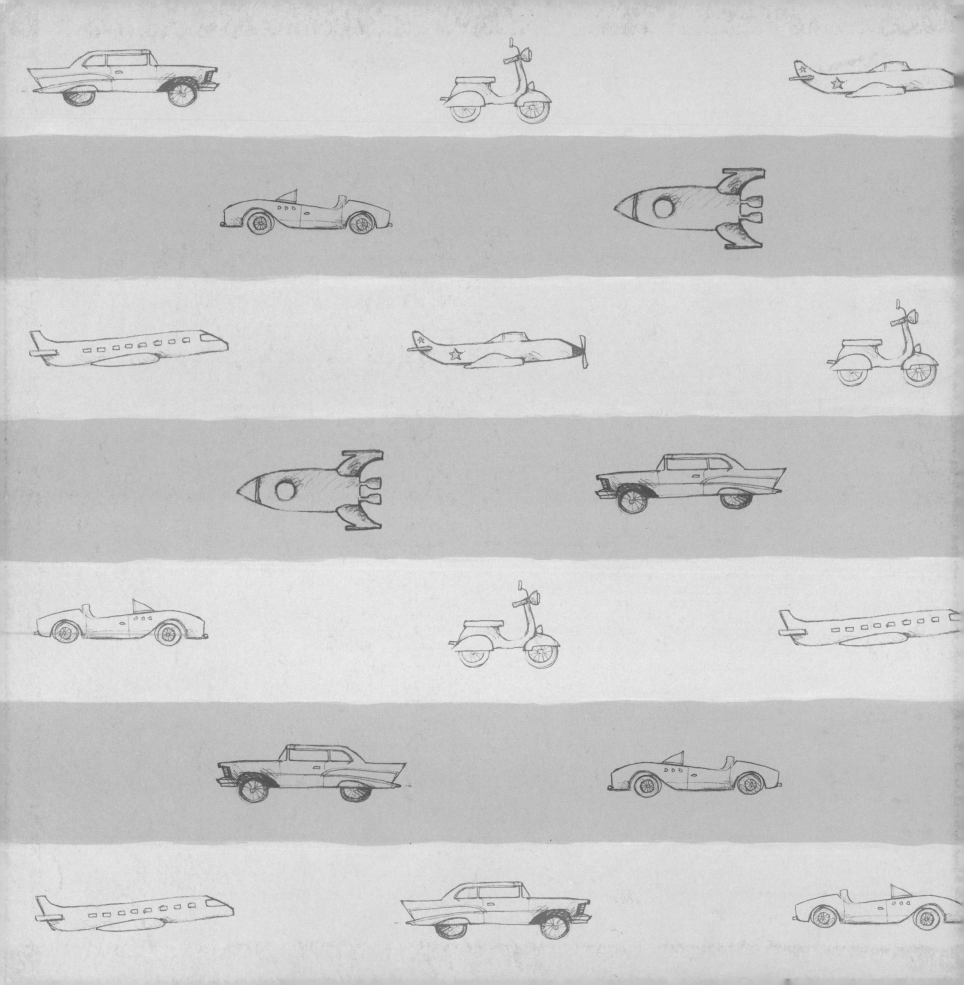